FIRST STEPS IN

WHAT'S AN ALGORITHM?

A SPLASH PARK ADVENTURE!

BY KAITLYN SIU AND MARCELO BADARI

Kane Miller

A DIVISION OF EDC PUBLISHING

First American Edition 2022
Kane Miller, A Division of EDC Publishing

Copyright © Hodder and Stoughton, 2022
First published in Great Britain in 2022
by Wayland, an imprint of Hachette Children's Group,
part of Hodder and Stoughton, Carmelite House,
50 Victoria Embankment, London EC4Y 0DZ

All rights reserved.
For information contact:
Kane Miller, A Division of EDC Publishing
5402 S 122nd E Ave
Tulsa, OK 74146

www.kanemiller.com
www.myubam.com

Library of Congress Control Number: 2021937021

Printed and bound in China
1 2 3 4 5 6 7 8 9 10
ISBN: 978-1-68464-334-9

FSC
www.fsc.org
MIX
Paper from
responsible sources
FSC® C104740

WHAT'S AN ALGORITHM?

Let's find out! It's time to go on a splash park adventure with two amazing robot friends. We'll have lots of fun and learn awesome coding skills with Jet and Bolt. Come on, super coders!

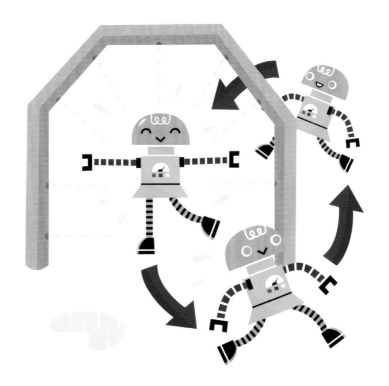

Jet and Bolt are super robots.
They have superpowers.
They can run fast, jump high,
and spin at super speed!

Jet and Bolt love having fun at the park. Jet can go up and down the slide 20 times in one minute! Bolt can swing so high he goes upside down!

The park is so much fun for robot friends.

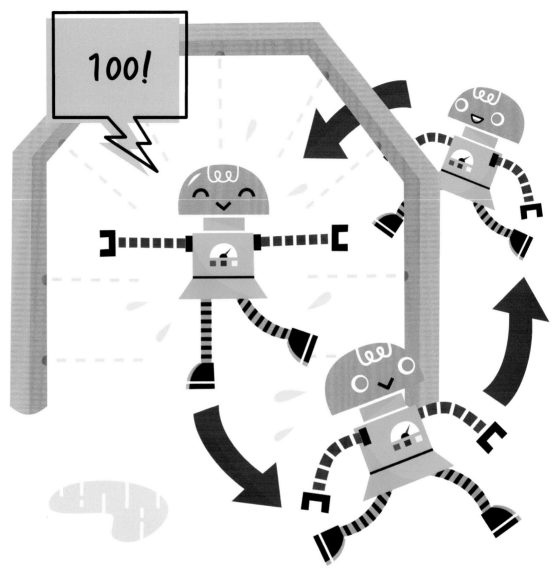

In the hot summer, Jet loves playing at the splash park.

She can't wait to run through the sprinkler 100 times in two minutes!

Jet wants to invite Bolt to
join her at the splash park.

She calls Bolt and asks him
to come and play.

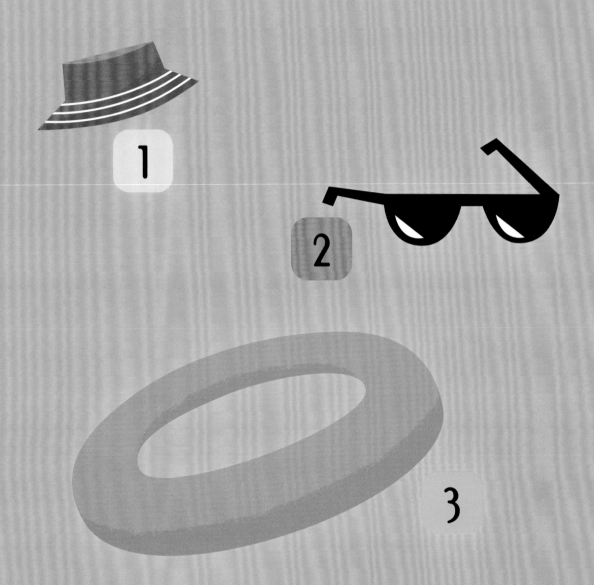

1

2

3

Bolt would love to go to the splash park!

He puts on his sun hat, sunglasses, and floatie. He is all dressed and ready to go.

But wait! Bolt doesn't know how to get to the splash park. He needs **directions** from his friend Jet.

Bolt needs an **algorithm** to find his way to the splash park.

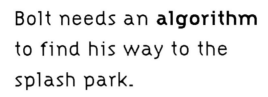

An algorithm?

What's that?

An algorithm is a set of **instructions** to help someone complete a **task**.

Algorithms help us **solve** problems by breaking them down into steps.

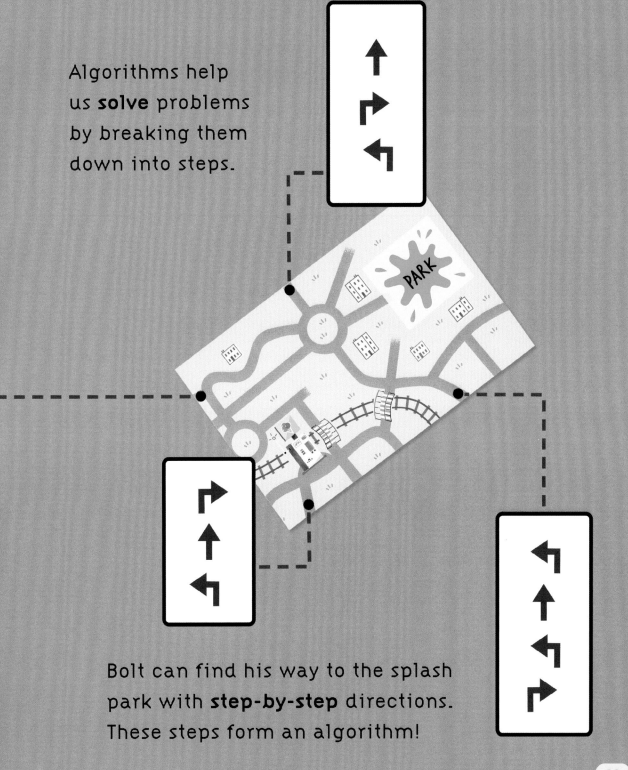

Bolt can find his way to the splash park with **step-by-step** directions. These steps form an algorithm!

Learning about algorithms is actually quite simple. An algorithm is just a plan for solving a problem.

Jet and Bolt use algorithms every day, just like you!

When we brush our teeth, we use our "teeth-brushing algorithm."

Imagine telling a robot exactly how you brush your teeth every day. You'll need to break it down, step-by-step.

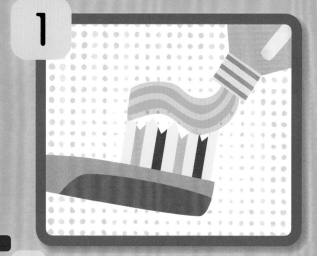

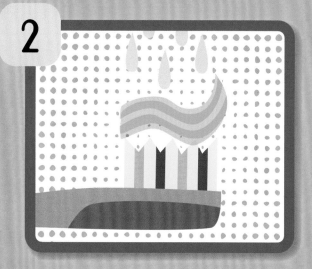

3

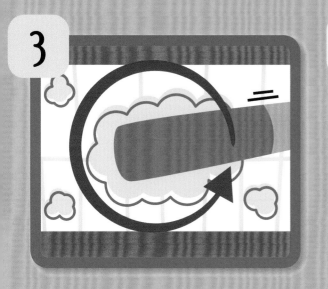

4

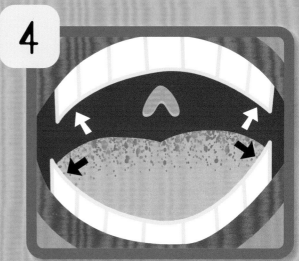

5

6

Why don't you try it now, out loud?
Explain to a friend exactly how you
brush your teeth. Don't forget any steps!

Jet sends an algorithm to help Bolt get to the splash park.

Step one: Leave the house.

Step two: Head straight toward the mailbox.

Step three: Turn right at the mailbox.

Step four: Go forward toward the stop sign.

Step five: Turn left at the stop sign.

Step six: Head toward the garden.

Step seven: Turn right at the garden.

Step eight: Use the bridge to cross over the train tracks.

Step nine: Follow the signs to the splash park!

SPLASH PARK →

With these directions,
Bolt will have no
problem finding
his way.

Bolt heads out along the path
toward the splash park.
He can't wait to try the
slippery slide!

SPLASH
PARK

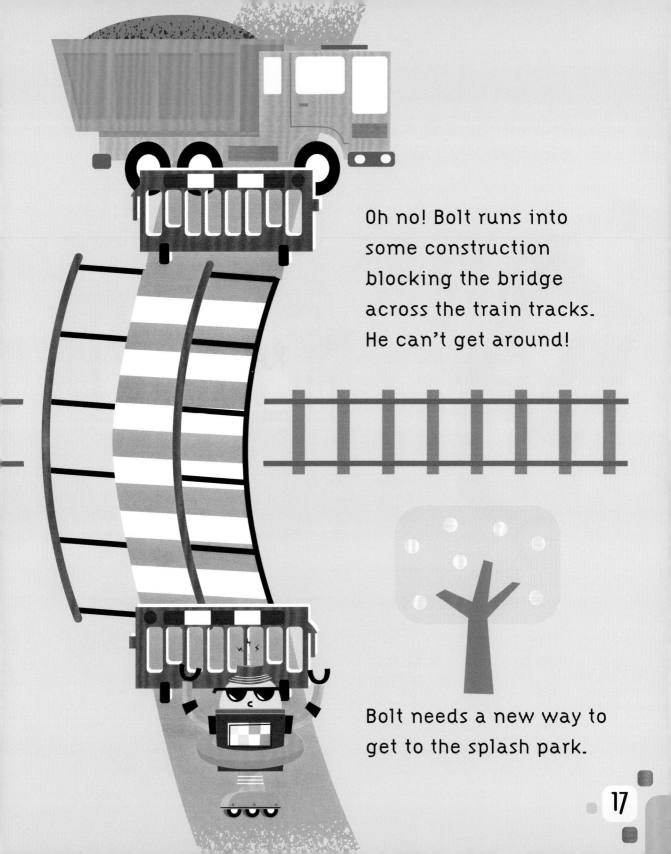

Oh no! Bolt runs into some construction blocking the bridge across the train tracks. He can't get around!

Bolt needs a new way to get to the splash park.

Bolt has found a mistake in Jet's algorithm.
He can't follow her steps because the route is
blocked. We call mistakes in algorithms **bugs**.

Real bugs??

No, these aren't real bugs!
Bugs are problems in our
instructions that we
need to fix. When
we fix a bug, we
call it **debugging**.

We can help Bolt get to the
splash park by debugging
Jet's algorithm.

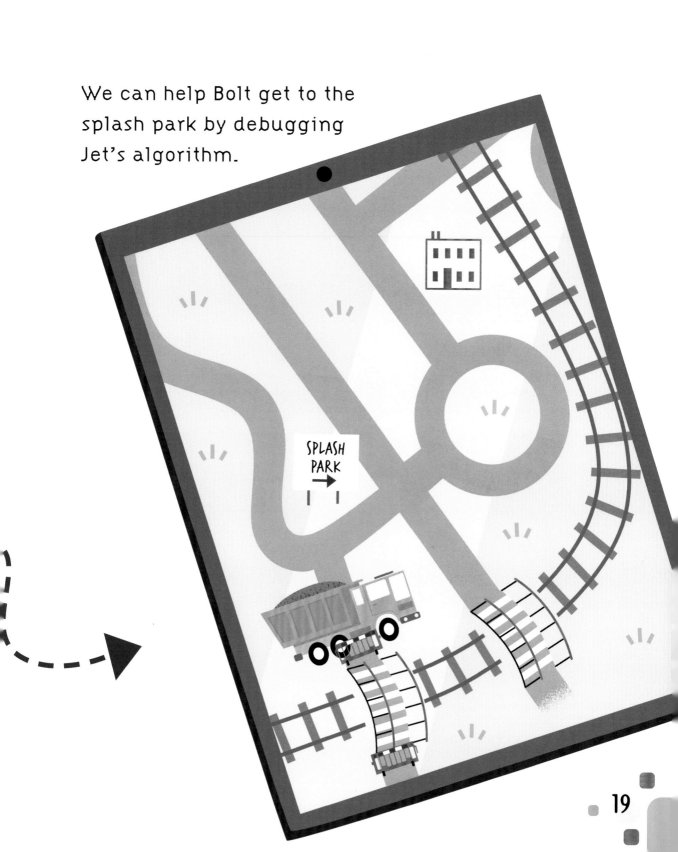

Let's find a way around. Which way do you
think Bolt should go?

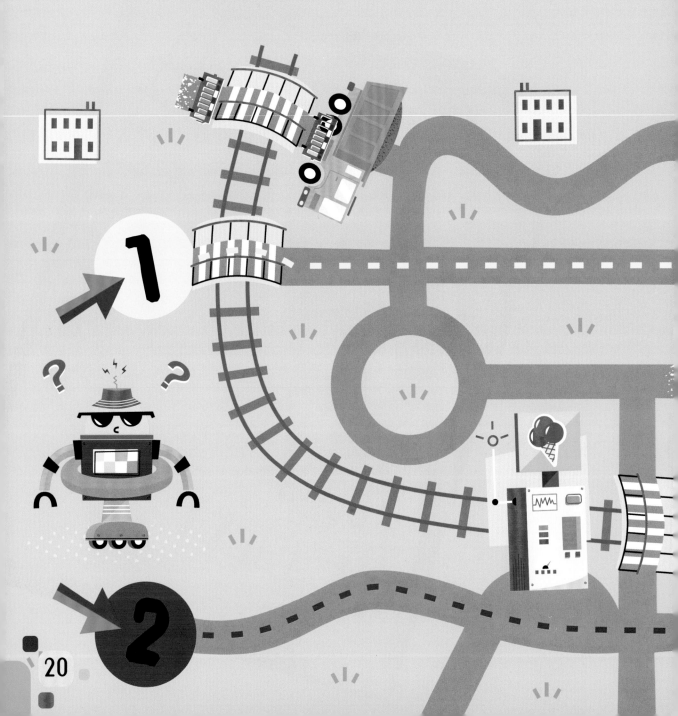

Choose Route 1 or Route 2.

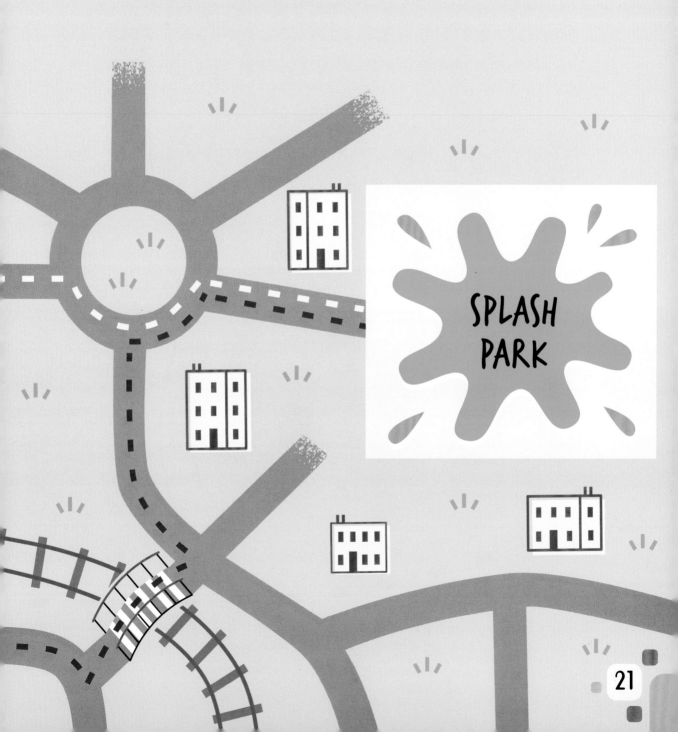

SPLASH PARK

When making an algorithm, we can choose
to make it for the shortest and quickest route,
or we can make it for a longer route that stops
at an ice cream shop. Yum!

We can set our algorithm to be whatever
we choose, to follow whatever path we like
to get to the finish line.

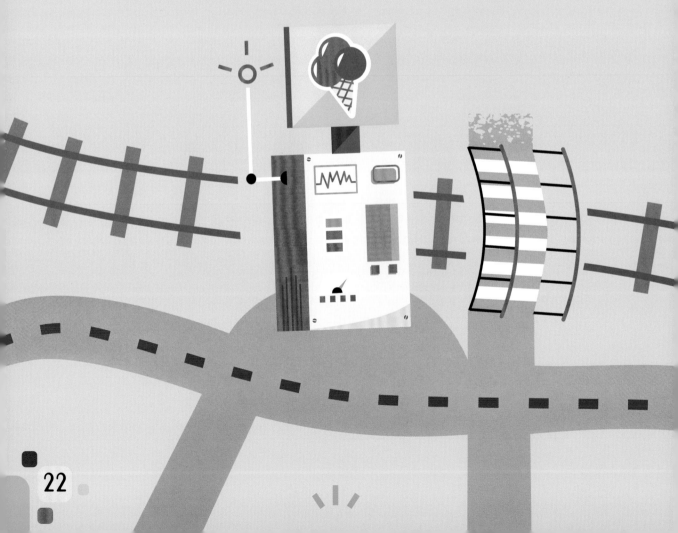

Bolt is back on his way to the splash park!

Finally, Bolt has made it to the splash park! The debugged algorithm worked.

PARK ENTRANCE

He spins in the water so fast that he creates a huge wave!

Jet loves playing with Bolt in the water.

Getting to the splash park was easy once we debugged and found a good algorithm.

Algorithms are simple instructions that help us complete a task.

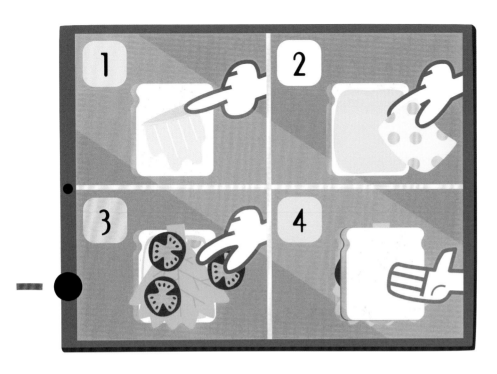

Can you think of other ways
we use algorithms every day?

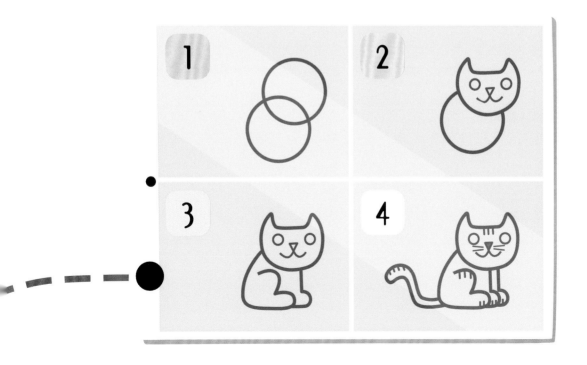

Now it's your turn! Design your own algorithm.

Can you find the fastest way for Jet to get home from the splash park?

SPLASH PARK

Use your finger to trace a path along the white lines from the splash park to Jet's house. Watch out for the objects blocking the path!

As you move your finger, list your instructions in order.

JET'S HOUSE

29

GLOSSARY

bug: a problem or mistake in coding instructions

debug: find and solve a problem in coding instructions

direction: the way something moves along a specific path

instruction: information that tells us what to do

step-by-step: following a set of instructions one at a time

solve: find an answer to a problem

task: a job to be done

GUIDE FOR TEACHERS, PARENTS, AND CAREGIVERS

Young children can learn the basic concepts of coding. These concepts are the foundation of computer science, as well as other important skills, such as critical thinking and problem-solving.

In this book, readers learn all about how to create their own algorithm. We use the concept of a set of instructions giving directions to explain this task. An algorithm is an instruction given in order to complete a certain task and receive the desired result.

So, a computer programmer writes an algorithm to tell the computer how to perform a certain task to produce a required result.

INDEX

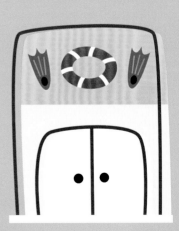